Glances Through The Eyes Of The Reaper

PAUL S. HUGGINS

Copyright © 2017 Paul S. Huggins

All rights reserved.

ISBN: 1545416257
ISBN-13: 978-1545416259

DEDICATION

For Sally.

Without whom I would be nothing.
She is my universe.

CONTENTS

	Acknowledgments	i
1	The Last Sunrise	1
2	Ghost Hunt	16
3	The Family Business	17
4	Message in a Bottle	20
5	Cold Valentine	21
6	Grease Paint	28
7	The Meek	29
8	A Drink a Day	32
9	The Tower	33
10	Dead	35
11	Night Terror	36
12	Abandoned Luggage	40
13	Divided but United	41
14	No Job Satisfaction	50
15	Dawn of the Triffids	51

ACKNOWLEDGMENTS

Dawn of the Triffids First published in "The Many moods of David Moody".

1 THE LAST SUNRISE

The leaves of the solitary oak tree rustled and jostled in the warm, dry wind. The branches rose and dropped almost with a rhythmic oscillation. Looking up from the ground the crisp dry, dead foliage silhouetted against a cloudless crystal blue sky still looked alive in the shaded relief.

Scarlet was twenty five, she felt fifteen again as she lay recumbent on her back gazing up through the once mighty tree branches. A time when the limbs on which the leaves hung would have been green, and life would have been in them.

Her roughly shorn black hair was a stark contrast to her pale Goth like complexion created by layer upon layer of sun cream. She raised her right arm in a broad arc sweeping the smoking cigarette that she held, towards her mouth. With a pout she gently kissed the already drained filter tip. Her chest rose as she inhaled the nicotine tainted smoke deeply. She had to enjoy this final smoke as it was the very last of her stockpile.

Scarlet pushed herself up onto her elbows. The change in view made the happier memories of a more innocent time fade and dissipate. She took another drag on the cigarette and this time blew the cloud towards the inanimate body that lay just a few feet from her and the dead tree.

She gazed without remorse at the body of the man she had murdered less than ten minutes earlier. The grubby denims, the lumberjack shirt with sleeves rolled up to the elbow, the tattered military combat boots. His stone face belied his thirty something years, chiseled weather worn features were partially obscured by a short beard growth. His mussed hair was matted, and sandy, with grime and natural grease from lack of cleansing.

The cigarette was almost a stub. Scarlet looked past the corpse and took in the open expanse of the plane beyond. Within the horizon thin tendrils of dark smoke signaled where a city had once stood, London, Manchester, Glasgow, it could have been any one of them, the few people left had forgotten which. The broken and jagged derelict tower blocks were the same sandy hue as the surrounding arid countryside.

She knew the world could not survive for very much longer. She felt the loneliest that she ever had, even after the war when families and friends were maliciously torn away it did not compare to the hopelessness of the present. She believed there was no God, there was barely man. If he created man in his own image then it went to follow, that he was dead or dying too. After all it was the deity's supporters that had caused this mess in the first place.

It had been after years of conflict around the

globe. On both religious and moral grounds the people of the first world had finally put the planet on course for total annihilation. Ever since the industrial revolution mankind had raped and pillaged the earth's resources, even its atmosphere now bereft of the ability to refresh itself had suffered at the hands of men.

In less than two hundred years, evolution had been extinguished in one foul swoop by the very smallest of molecules in the universe, the atom. The religious right, in its wisdom, unleashed the power of fission on its foes. They exacted destruction in the name of the almighty and in their minds acted as if they were the hand of God.

The first few years after the war were a maelstrom of nuclear winter, it killed off much of the life that had been previously lucky (or unlucky) enough to survive the initial onslaught. Despite the TS Elliot saying 'This is the way the World ends, not with a bang but a whimper.' Man will go out with a whimper.' Man really did go out with a bang, one comparable to that of the big bang of creation. Not only had life on earth become a rarity, the planet itself was nearing the point of being erased from existence.

The power of the plethora of nuclear explosions, weapons that coincidently had no longer existed according to the United Nations inspectorate, not only destroyed life and society but had also done irreparable damage to the earth's axis.

The planet was spiraling out of its orbit path around the sun, and was now headed in a slow arc toward it. The seasons had gone from spring, summer, autumn and winter to become one long summer of only slightly varying degrees, with the occasional monsoon like storm to break up the monotony of the dry heat for but a moment. Days were long, the shortest having a mere four hours of night, even then it was still light enough not to need luminescent assistance to get around. For the other ten or eleven months of the year night was a forgotten concept.

The continents had enlarged considerably, the seas and oceans having dried up to dramatic levels. The Mediterranean was no more than a large saltwater swamp. It was even possible, with time and stamina, to walk across the English Channel to France.

Not that any of the few humans left would try. Self-preservation was the order of the day. Governments collapsed, as did regional councils, the military, and then finally local militias. There were no longer any rules and regulations.

People led a solitary hand to mouth existence, mostly underground, awaiting the inevitable. As the months and years passed the sun's rays became stronger, and more powerful, penetrating deeper into the earth's crust with every passing day. The greens, greys and browns of nature had become the yellows, tans and oranges of an arid desert wasteland.

Scarlet breathed out the last remnants of smoke. She inspected the burnt out stub of the now dead cigarette, like her it was barely clinging to life. With one final wisp of smoke the last strand of aging dry tobacco became ash and the cigarette did finally die. She rolled the dog end between thumb and forefinger, then flicked it with malice at the man laid out before her.

Trust was an outdated concept. It had morphed itself from a word to describe a truthful reliability, into gullibility, stupidity and death. Scarlet regarded anyone she met as the enemy, it is the reason she had survived for so long. As time progressed so too had the length of time between each encounter with another living being. Which announced to her that less people were surviving, this made any encounter all the more dangerous. Only the strong and most ruthless were left, the weak were gone in the aftermath of the old world and forgotten.

The man that lay dead before her was one of those strong people. He met his match when he crossed swords with Scarlet. Despite her slender frame and average height, she was an Amazonian warrior that would have put Boadicea to shame.

She was a master at fighting with a baton style police night stick, the handled short staff generally favoured by the US police, and a modern adoption of the British Bobbies truncheon. She was also very fit due to when she was growing up she was always in the dance studio or gymnasium. As a result she was balanced, fast and above all disciplined. Nobody left carried guns anymore. With the temperature rising the carrying of explosives in your pocket would have been suicide, in fact carrying any form of self-igniting item was dangerous. Fighting had returned to a more base level, equal to medieval times. The futuristic weapons, such as long distance sniper rifles, laser guided drones and Apache attack helicopters, were consigned to a forgotten past. You looked your opponent right in the eye, it was one on one.

Due to the heat, battles were not long drawn out affairs like the choreographed scenes in action movies. These warriors were, fast and strong, they went in hard and fast, battles barely lasted a minute.

Despite having rested for a quarter of an hour at most, Scarlet was still recovering. Her method was one of surprise, swiftly removing her baton which was slung behind her underneath her parka. She would, in one fluid motion, pull it from her left side and reign a tirade of blows on her attacker. The majority of the people left were right handed, attacking from her left most often caught them by surprise as the majority expected attack from the right.

She got lucky with the fight she had just ended. She came out of her corner with a glancing blow of the man's right shoulder taking him totally by surprise, he had reeled and dipped his head forward. With the follow through she brought the weapon down on the back of his head with an almighty crack.

Just two hits and the man fell dead on impact to the ground. For him, a merciful release, especially for her as he was much taller and stronger. When they first crossed paths he had made his intentions crystal clear as to what he wanted from her. All her food and water, then for dessert a piece of her. He barely had the time to register he had picked on the wrong girl, before his life was ended.

Scarlet grunted as she pushed herself up to a standing position. The slither of sun that covered the entire eastern horizon was already strong enough to feel its warmth on her cheek. Close to the tree lay her small, but adequate, back pack. She picked it up daintily and pulled it onto her shoulders slinging the night stick on its side as she did. With one last glance she regarded the body with distain and headed down the hillock away from the tree. Once on the arid plain she picked a direct route to the once mighty hub of capitalism. It was now the centre of her world and where her hideout was located. In her childhood that city had been her home.

She followed the dusty tracks that crossed and intersected all over the flat countryside. The space had once been fields of lush well irrigated corn, despite being the same yellow hue nothing lived there anymore, the soil was dry and bereft of nutrients.

She stopped, a frown on her face. To the west a small dark movement drew her attention. If it had been a few hours later she would have put it down to heat haze or hallucinations caused by dehydration.

She studied it, tried to figure out what it was. A slight deviation in its progress made her realize the figure was moving. Its approach directly towards her made its movement undetectable at the distance it was away from her. The frown became a grimace as it now appeared to be a humanlike figure, albeit completely shrouded in a black cloak or blanket.

It was not unusual to be wearing a dark covering, especially if you were unfortunate enough to get caught outside during the day. When the sun was high in the sky UV protection was paramount, unless the daytime traveler had a perverse liking of third degree burns.

Scarlet moved on and picked up her pace. She ensured she kept the figure within her peripheral vision, it was continuing its route towards her, but was still some distance away. She reached the edge of the once bustling city. Within the confines of its welcoming shade she felt more at home. Its collapsing skyscrapers and derelict tenements were blending in well with the rest of the landscape.

The buildings were more reminiscent of dunes, cliffs and mountains than once busy offices and houses. Dust and sand had filled open doorways and glassless windows. As a child Scarlet had wondered what the world would be like if man just upped and left. Now she knew first hand. As she entered the well-trodden path she had travelled many times before, she glanced back and found, to her horror the figure was closing the gap between them.

It was almost certainly a person, despite being completely shrouded in black, it seemed un-naturally tall. The vision chilled her to the bone, but she could not put her finger on why.

She slipped along the streets, now no more than tracks in dust, a layer so thick that the concrete and tar would never be seen again. She took twists and turns in the hope it would prevent her pursuer from following her to the hideout.

Being on familiar ground Scarlet's curiosity needed to be satisfied and her best chance to get a look at the odd figure would be to get to higher ground. In the part of town she was in there were high-rise tower blocks aplenty. She knew her way round and finding an accessible one wouldn't be too much of a problem.

She ducked along vacated alleys and back roads, then she veered left heading for a derelict block that she holed up in before the daytime heat had forced her underground. It was four stories high, but had originally been six. Constant weathering had reduced its top two levels to rubble that was now strewn across its new roof. She headed for what used to be her regular access point.

Next to a window the shell of a car was a semi-permanent fixture, its paintwork scorched off over the years, leaving bare, pitted metal. Scarlet stepped onto the trunk, then onto the roof, finally pulling herself in through the hollow, empty window frame. Despite its dark mustiness, the interior was not much different from outside, the dust had a habit of getting into the smallest of nooks.

The internal staircase was bare concrete but still intact enough to use and led her straight up to the roof, the steps terminated into space. Scarlet picked her way through the debris and made herself comfortable and partly hid herself by some of the larger weathered blocks.

From her vantage point she could see a large swathe of the derelict suburb. A few streets over, she could just make out the start of the desert plain. The building she now perched on like a roosting pigeon had, most likely been, a multi-level shop. Its frontage opened up onto what was once a busy through route into the heart of the city. It was now a glorified foot track, although less and less travelled in recent months.

Scarlet leaned out, eager to look back in the direction that the dark figure would most likely come. As if on cue he strolled into her field of vision. Scarlet pulled back into cover and clandestinely watched him approach. The figure intrigued her. There were two strange things she had noticed about him, her or it.

Firstly the movement was so steady, it reminded her of how an air hockey puck would float over the table on its cushion of air. More disturbingly was that the figure looked to be at least eight feet tall. She watched in silence as the figure passed her by, way below her. Not before stopping for a moment when directly beneath her position.

Scarlet held her breath. After just a few seconds that felt like minutes the figure moved on. She waited until he had disappeared from sight before she left her hiding place. She descended the building and stepped out onto the deserted street.

It was certainly time for her to take refuge, she felt the heat increasing as the dawn approached. It felt to her that it was going to be a furnace of a day. Scarlet looked in all directions as she headed across what used to be a road and joined a track that would eventually lead her to her hiding place. The tall stranger added paranoia to her haste to get home.

The temperature seemed to increase with every few steps she took, the air was also becoming thinner as the oxygen was beginning to burn out of it. Dawn had come far earlier than Scarlet had estimated it would.

After slipping down another sheltered alleyway she emerged into a back road that gave access to the rear gardens of the houses that backed onto it. This road terminated at a dead end with a brick wall.

A 'V' shaped gap in the wall was her entry point into the wide space on the other side. She turned sideways to get through the fissure. The open area on the other side had once been a park, somewhere Scarlet had loved when a child. The boating lake was now a slight dip in the surrounding desert, it had once been filled with carp, and Scarlet remembered with fondness how she had fed the ducks as a shy preteen with her father and little brother. The surrounding park area had been filled with greenery and every type of tree. Borders and flowerbeds added to the natural colour and scents.

Not far from the gap was the entrance to her hiding place, a Victorian white brick built shed, it had once been hidden amongst the trees. It now stood up like the buildings left standing at ground zero of Hiroshima after the Americans had exacted their revenge for Pearl Harbour in 1945.

Her skin that was uncovered tingled as the first unfiltered rays from the sun touched it. She pulled her parka around her more tightly in an effort to shade herself, something she was well practiced at. She was virtually there and didn't need to rush.

A stripped bare rusted sign gave little away as to the curious buildings use. She pulled at the handle of the steel riveted door adjacent to it. With a groan and grind the door gave and continued opening with little effort.

Scarlet entered, but as she turned to close it behind her she froze. Standing, not forty feet away, in the rubble of the wall through which she had just passed stood the tall black figure.

Her instinct kicked in and she slammed the door shut. Her hand groped around at the edge of it, as if well practiced she found her quarry and slammed the metal bar in the recesses either side barricading herself within. Guided by the strips of light shining in through gaps in the roof she located the manhole cover and slid it open. Sitting on its edge, she dangled her feet inside, taking the weight on her arms lowered herself until her feet met a rung of a metal ladder. She climbed down a few treads then pulled the heavy metal cover back into place from below. The darkness was consuming. She continued down to the bottom, a complete drop of around ten feet. She groped again, this time behind the ladder. The large box of matches had to stay below ground as they would ignite from the heat if allowed above ground, next to them she retrieved a torch fashioned from dry solid timber and grass.

Due to the lessening of oxygen it was sometimes hard to keep one of these burning torches alight. Today was no exception and it took three matches and more dry grass to coax a low flame from it. A sign on the opposite side of the ladder announced a warning to be wary of electrical cabling, gas build ups and steam evacuations. It also warned that the borough council would not be held responsible for any injury caused due to unauthorized entry into the sewer system.

Luckily for Scarlet the gas pipes had been purged during the war, the copper of the electrical cabling had become green and nonconductive and the steam pipes were cold.

She expected to hear pounding on the door before she got the manhole cover back in place, but she had heard nothing, she had the ethereal feeling that the figure was waiting, and watching her.

She walked along the tunnel as it gently sloped downward. Her footsteps echoed but apart from that and the occasional crackle from the torch there was nothing to be heard. She was a little uneasy, the familiar coolness of the sewer system was replaced by warmth, this made her nervous, as it meant the ground was heating down further than it ever had before.

After more downward ladders and a couple of refreshed torches from her stockpiles throughout the maze of tunnels she finally reached the place she called home. A hardwood door set into a tunnel wall opened with ease because of its greased hinges.

The room had originally been a rest place created during building of the system in the Victorian era.

Tunnel workers would spend days on shifts in the depths and this would have been where they ate, rested and slept.

At present it was more like an Aladdin's cave of non-perishable food and drink. Right in the middle was a military style camp bed, Scarlets bed. No covers adorned it just a heavily sweat stained pillow, a teddy bear and a wallet.

She closed the door behind her, dropped her pack at the foot of the bed, and slumped slowly onto it. She was exhausted after both fight and flight. She lay back and rested her head on the pillow. She looked up at the ceiling stained with long forgotten water marks. The truth be told those marks reminded her of a time when water was plentiful. She realized then that she was sweating, she sat up. It was definitely warm, something that it had never been in the past, she could normally rely on the coolness of her underground safe haven to make her feel a little more comfortable.

Her mouth was dry, she swallowed, and it hurt. She looked around and located her dwindling supply of water. She always refilled during monsoon time, which usually happened a couple of times a year. From what she could remember it had been a long time since the last one.

The heat seemed to continue increasing, it was up to the point of being uncomfortable. Worrying for Scarlett was that the day had only just begun. It was going to get hotter as the day wore on, to make matters worse there was nowhere to go that was deeper. As the sweat flowed the strength ebbed from her body. She drank greedily at a bottle of water, but it did not cool her or quench her thirst.

She lay back and gripped her threadbare teddy. She opened the wallet, there was only one item within. A photograph. With damp fingers she removed it carefully from the aging, cracked leather, it had been her fathers.

The photo was a little faded but she could still make out the four people in it. A couple, entwined in each other's arms with two small children in front of them, everybody was smiling with natural happiness. She remembered the day the picture was taken, it was on the beach at Hunstanton, and the fairground was still vaguely visible in the background. It had been the happiest day of her life. To her dismay the picture slowly darkened until the whole image became black. The chemicals within the photographic paper had reacted with the heat and it had become scorched.

She looked up, tears mingling with the perspiration stinging her eyes. Standing in the doorway was the dark figure. She was no longer concerned, it all made sense. She knew who this figure was. It was obvious. The collector of souls, the grim reaper, death himself, it was her time and there was no avoiding the inevitable.

The figure slowly lifted the hood of its cloak and revealed its face. With a shake of the head the familiar smile of her father was revealed.

'It's time to go my little Scarlet.' He said in a soft voice.

Scarlet returned the smile and with great effort slowly nodded her head. She laid back and closed her eyes. As she drifted away into unconsciousness she was unaware that she had been the very last person left alive on Earth.

With Scarlet dead, the human race had become

extinct. The planet was silent as the temperature continued to rise. The last shreds of man's existence burnt and melted. The deserts became lakes and rivers of molten glass.

As the sun climbed higher, and its rays penetrated deeper than previously, a reaction occurred between the super-heated Earth's surface and its own magmatic core. Close to the sun a new glowing star was born into the solar system.

2 GHOST HUNT

I crept around the abandoned mansion, following an impromptu amateur ghost hunt, in an allegedly haunted house. The girls screamed at an ear piercing pitch and the men stifled their own, equally girlish cries, to save face, I understand.

Every corner held shadows and mystery. A bottomless chair, a stained folded mattress, a broken toilet bowl, they all cast animate shadows that danced in the torch light.

I kept to the rear, not scared, never screaming. I followed, amused by the party.

I leaned in close, unbeknownst to the trailing hunter. Just one whisper and the panic will boil over.

3 THE FAMILY BUSINESS

The package arrived at noon. Jane stubbed out her cigarette butt into an already overflowing ashtray in the center of her kitchen table. The delivery had been expected to arrive at some point in her life; when was always the mystery. With her forefinger she whisked a few stray strands of her chestnut hair from her eyes and back round behind her ear. She exhaled deeply and expelled a plume of smoke.

She had always known her destiny had been preordained since before her birth, before her father was born.

Three sharp knocks on the door broke the peace. She paused then looked sternly into her palms before pushing the chair away and standing. Jane looked at the cigarette packet, she took one, lit it and then took a deep drag as if it was the first cigarette of the day, in reality it was her second pack of the day. Cigarette in mouth she went to the front door and opened it with a sharp crack of the handle.

Nobody was present but at her feet the expected

parcel sat. It was the size of a cereal box and lay perpendicular with the edge of the step, as if placed with perfect precision and a modicum of obsessive compulsion. The wrapping crackled as she gently lifted the box, the wax seal at the centre glistening in the sunlight, she closed the door and returned to the kitchen.

She placed it on the table with care and retook her seat. Calmly, she picked up the cool steel of a preplaced paring knife and broke the red seal on the package. She then removed the sandy coloured waxen paper and stared at the box it had been encapsulating.

Her unemotional face softened and she removed the hardwood lid. Nestled within the scarlet velvet material sat the leather bound tome, one of many billions that she knew existed. She caressed it with her finger tips feeling every pore of the rich leather grain, it was her first. The cool gold of the immaculate locking mechanism on the edge of the cover glinted from the sunlight which poured through the kitchen window.

She removed the book from the box and discarded the packaging. She positioned the book in front of her on the table. She tilted her head forward and searched through the hair at the back of her neck. Her fingers swiftly found her quarry. She unclipped the hasp of the gold chain and removed her necklace. She held it in front of her and took a hold of the small golden key that dangled from it.

Using the key she unlocked the clasp of the book and it released silently. Jane turned the ornate cover. The title page read 'The life of Jeremy Hodson'. The woman nodded in understanding blowing smoke to the right. She turned the thick vellum sheet and

'Contents' appeared heading the next page.

One line of text was displayed, the only line required. It read, 'Page 358. Chapter 144: The End'. She flicked through the book, the pages would have been blank but for the numbering, until she reached her goal, Page 358. Jane began to read the couple of paragraphs displayed.

'1:18 pm. Jeremy left the house, his car had seen better days but he desperately needed to travel. As he negotiated a set of traffic lights another car came from nowhere and broadsided his own. Jeremy suffered, but not for long as both vehicles erupted into a ball of flame caused by Jeremy's leaking fuel system. The occupants of both vehicles were incinerated beyond recognition.'

Her destiny was written, she looked up at the clock to see that it was 12:15, she had just over an hour. She locked and repackaged the book. After placing her necklace with it, she attached a fresh address label. She rose from her chair, and grabbed her car keys as she left the house with the package under her arm.

Jane Reaper had waited her entire life to have a hand in the family business, the time was nigh for her to work with the rest of her relatives. For Grim Reaper Incorporated business was booming.

4 MESSAGE IN A BOTTLE

Sarah strolled along the shore, as she did most evenings since her retirement. Something caught her eye in the ebb and flow at the water's edge.

As she approached she saw that it was a bottle. She picked it up, its lid was screwed tight and labels gone. Inside she could just make out, through the frosted glass, a rolled up piece of paper. Sarah took a moment to extract the note:

'To whoever finds this message, I hope you have a happy life. Signed Sarah (age 8)'

She smiled to herself as the sun disappeared over the western horizon.

5 COLD VALENTINE

It was Valentine's Day, a day I would never forget in a hurry. I was a bookbinder at the time; shift work was unavoidable. On this particular day, I was on the early shift. Early shifts were six in the morning for twelve hours, not much time for anything but work, especially with a forty-five minute ride in on my motorcycle. It was tiresome getting up at five in the morning. This morning I had been happy and bushy tailed for once, mainly as I had something out of the ordinary to do on my way to work.

At the end of our road, just where the modern estate started, lived a cute girl with her parents. She was quite a babe. Not only was she beautiful but also pleasant and intelligent with it. I had known her for years, pretty much watched her grow up. There was a couple of years between us but that's not too important when you are in your late teens as we both were.

I also knew her boyfriend. Not the shiniest apple in the cart, for that matter popularity and looks eluded him as well. Going by the arguments I had seen between them he did not really respect her too much either. For these reasons I knew she would be better off with someone who would appreciate and love her, me.

There was a large manila envelope waiting on the hall table, marked with her name and ready for delivery.

It was a cold morning that February 14th. Two Jerseys and a scarf under my bike jacket on this day. As I left the house in the darkness of the early hours the road outside was effervescing with a pure white frost that would probably be gone in the following couple of hours.

Icy roads are not great for two-wheel riding. It was only a glorified moped. If I still owned it the thing would be quite rare at present and probably worth far more than it was back then. It was a Simson 51, which was an East German manufactured bike whose company went bust in 2003.

When it was running, it had been superb; sadly, it spent more time back in the dealers than on the road. Despite it being only a moped it still managed a steady top speed of about 50mph, but not in the condition of the road on that day.

The bike was a little unusual in its operation; the ignition key went into the side, just behind my thigh, a very odd position. The key also operated the lights, by turning it further round when required. The style was a sort of on/off roader, comfortable on the road, looked like it should be just as happy off road with its high-level exhaust and mudguards, in reality it was really only any good on the flat level tarmac.

It started fine for a change so after a couple of

minutes warming up I headed on up the crystal glinting road, using incredible care. Within seconds, I pulled up and left the bike idling while I nipped up the path and posted the card through the front door of the end of terrace house.

With my personal job done it was now off to continue travelling to work. I took it nice and steady, it was dark and thankfully too early for any other traffic to be out yet. I prefer that as I think most motorcyclists will agree. If you do get in trouble and slide off due to ice, diesel or just plain wet, you do not want some idiot in his centrally heated metal box so infused by his music or on the phone that he drives right over you.

It was going to be a long journey. The roads out of town were not quite so frosty, but I still kept it steady and slow. I started into a small town that was just three miles into my twenty-mile journey. The orange glow of the streetlights lit up the central point of the village. It was a large hexagonal thatched shelter known locally as the fountain. From this point on the road became virtually single lane due to all the cars parked along its kerbs.

It seemed to get icy again as I left the long row of parked cars behind and approached the edge leading out of the town. The last bend had been ahead, it was a sharp right-hander. It turned onto an old stone bridge. I slowed down to a walking pace as the road reflected ominously in the streetlights.

I started to turn carefully as the bridge came into view I realised the glinting reflection from the road had been sheet ice. As I committed around the corner the grip on the rubber tyres was lost in an instant. The front slid out, I panicked and put down my right foot.

The ice was so prevalent I might as well have been riding on a sheet of glass. The front wheel continued to slide out and as I could not get a footing that also slid in the same direction.

All was lost as myself and the bike fell. I hit the road hard on my right side. There was an audible crack. I lay for a few seconds with the bike under my legs. Something did not feel right. I dragged myself out from under the bike slightly panicked because if a car came round the corner I would have been right in its way. My right arm was useless and I could not straighten my head up.

Nobody was about at this early hour. I had certainly broken something, but at the time was not sure what. I knew shock would set in soon, I already felt a little groggy. With my right arm held tight to my side and my head held over to the same side I Painfully struggled with just my left arm and managed to drag the bike onto the footpath.

I pulled the keys out and pocketed them. Anyone seeing me would have mistaken me for a zombie ambling back down the road the way I had come. It was still bitterly cold but I was starting to get warm. Back in those days mobile phones were not as affordable as they are now, I did not have one. I headed back to the fountain where the nearest payphone was.

Barely a single car passed me as I stumbled along. Once I reached the fountain I pushed my way into the phone box picked up the receiver and dropped a few coins in. I then tapped in the only number that came to mind.

It did not ring for very long and the sleepy voice of my mother answered.

"Hi Mum, I've had an accident. I think I broke my collar bone." I groaned.

"Why didn't you call an ambulance?" She replied.

After explaining where I was, she hung up and I took a seat in the adjacent hexagonal shelter to wait for her. While I waited, the shock kicked in with dizziness and heavy nausea. I did not have to wait long before my mums little blue sports car pulled up. She helped me into the car and took me to the nearest accident and emergency department. The doctors confirmed that I had indeed broken my collarbone.

It was a good couple of months before I was well enough to ride again. Not long after the bike finally gave up and died on me. As time passed I felt it quite ironic that as I tried to steal another man's girl, I am injured in an accident not half an hour later. Maybe karma does exist after all.

My Valentine travels do not stop there. It had been exactly a year later. I no longer worked at the bookbindery; I was doing a permanent nightshift cleaning up after gigs at a music venue. Some gigs were less arduous than others were, sometimes it would take two hours, and other times ten.

Although the events were still prevalent, the girl was still with the idiot. Just to add to my anxiety I left work at five in the morning and would be travelling the same stretch of road, crossing the same bridge, at about the same time. The only differences being a better bike and I would have been going in the opposite direction.

It had not been as cold as it had the previous year, but there was still a frost. I would be lying if I said I was not scared, I was borderline terrified. I was riding like a tortoise, a very slow one at that.

At a point just over half way home there is a stretch of road that we call the mad mile. It's a beautiful straight run of round about a mile, perfect for a fast run but not that night. I was pootling along at about 20mph.

Concentrating hard on the road ahead, I had not noticed a car approaching fast from behind. I swore as the silver saloon car flashed past me at incredible speed. A sweeping bend heralded the end of the mad mile. I approached it cautiously and turned even more carefully.

As I turned into the apex of the corner, I saw some lights shining out from the hedgerow. My initial thought was that it was early for a farmer to be cutting the hedges. As I got nearer, the realisation dawned on me that it was the speeder.

The wide grass verge had deep furrows passing in between two telegraph poles; they finally terminated at the car sitting sideways on in a ditch. I pulled up next to the verge. The tarmac was so slippery with ice I almost fell over getting off.

I rushed over to the stricken vehicle, which was wedged tight in the ditch, as I got closer I could hear the engine still running and surprisingly still revving up. I made it to the car just as another approaching vehicle slowed up and eased to a stop close to my bike. I looked in through the driver's side window to see the driver sitting trying to drive, changing gear from forward to reverse trying to move.

I banged on the window which he eventually opened a crack.

'What are you doing?' I shouted over the noise of the engine.

'It, it won't move.' He bleated.

'That might be because one of your wheels is over there.' I threw my hand in a pointing motion behind me.

Four burley men from the second car approached and I quickly and filled them in. They coaxed the shocked man from the wrecked car. The men agreed to give the guy a lift home, he only lived a mile or so away in the next village.

'Oh no not again, my wife is going to kill me.' The driver said as he was helped out of the wrecks window. That made us smile; lucky for him he was unhurt during the accident.

The rest of my journey was thankfully uneventful. Every 14th February I remember those two eventful rides and am very cautious every Valentine's Day. Especially when riding and whom I send cards to.

6 GREASE PAINT

Every day I have to wear this makeup. Grease paint reds, blues and white. I etch the garish smile on my face, from ear to ear. When in the ring, the children laugh, squeal and cheer. I know, deep down, they are laughing at me. The character out front is not what they see, it's just plain me. They laugh as I fall from my bicycle. They squeal as I trip over imagined obstacles. They cheer when the plank hits my head. The permanent smile never wavers. Deep down, in the soul of my being, I am crying and sobbing.

7 THE MEEK

Darkness was his friend, light was his enemy. Despite being forced to be a solitary creature by circumstance, he hankered for the experiences of the towns and cities of man, like all others of his breed. To be close to the activity of humans gave him joy to a degree, he bore witness to mankind. If seen by the people they would not understand that deep down the differences were minimal. They would hound him, abuse him and without a doubt kill him in a heartbeat.

He watched from the shadows, the safety of an underground retreat always a short hop or bolt from his position. There was no other creature on earth more passive and naturally un-invasive than he. The convenience that humans seemed to constantly yearn was as far from his thoughts as men are from their next neighbor planet in the solar system. Not that he was an alien, far from it.

He was of this Earth just as man, his kind were born long before man came down from the trees.

They existed with the dinosaurs, their instinct to hide was paramount. Unfortunately mankind overrules, abuses and destroys. Things that the figure in the shadows could not comprehend. Their constant expanding and destruction of nature's features and their hunger for the meat of the other planet dwellers upset him. His own diet mainly existed of moss and lichens, meat he did not hanker for nor could he digest. Feelings such as sadness and happiness only existed for him in a very mild way, he was a creature of constant fear that would vary in degrees. The constant overwhelming terror of being discovered and precipitating the end to the oldest inhabitants of what man thinks is his World.

Tonight the attraction was the bright lights, music and exotic smells coming from a street party. It was bright but shadows aided him aplenty.

He watched as children danced and chased each other around tables, stalls and bemused passersby. This part of human existence he relished, it pushed his fear down. He was transfixed by the jollity, the wide eyes and broad smiles of innocent fun.

His attention became transfixed, watching the happy spinning dancers caught him off guard and he did not realize he was at the furthest edge of the shadows. A shrill scream brought him back to reality. A man-child stood before him, her blond locks rattled by the cool night breeze. Her eyes were wide like the playful children but not with joy, they were fixed wide and in fear, at him.

She screamed again as the shouts and calls of men came to the fore. He leaped high, over the head of the catatonic child, ensuring he cleared her unharmed in an effort to reach the safety of a bolt hole. The hate and noise was all around him, closing in. He did not reach the comfort of utter darkness.

The men hit, they kicked, beat and tore at his grey leathery hide. Their hate overwhelmed him as his life ebbed away, the thoughts and fears inbred into him over the centuries were true. He bleated like a lamb which became shrill and high pitched. The sound ended as he died.

The shadows all around the World began to move and bustle as one. Unity was a concept man could not comprehend, they all knew that one of their own was gone. Retribution and retaliation was swift, and worldwide. By morning man was gone, in nine short hours' humankind was wiped clean of the planet, replaced by an older breed. A lifeform that no longer needed to hide in the shadows.

The meek inherited the Earth.

8 A DRINK A DAY

'A drink a day, to take the pain away' said the tramp to himself as he took yet another sip from the brown paper wrapped bottle. His eyelids felt heavy as he leaned back against the viaduct wall. It was his time, he was certain. As he drifted into unconsciousness the bottle slipped through the bag and out of his hand. It slid down his heavily clad thigh and rolled across the footpath. Its journey was halted by a black booted foot. The tall stranger stood over the hobo, a fire deep in his eyes. 'It is time, come.' He gestured.

9 THE TOWER

Standing at the top of the edifice made the whole world of hurt that got her to this point worthwhile. It had taken her a week of climbing to reach the pinnacle, but the terraced nature of the structure allowed for ample rest and rough sleeping when needed.

The tower was not dissimilar to the ancient Mayan temples of Mexico. Only this one was older, taller and located on the opposite side of the planet on the little explored Russian steppes.

The view was surreal, the perfect curve of the earth, mountains like ruffles in an ill laid carpet and the distant blue white blend of the ozone layer with the sky and the sea and the meeting of space. Move her it did not. It was worthwhile but only as an affirmation.

She cracked a half smile, she had expected a change, a confirmation that this was not all that life had for her. She wanted to believe that the last 35 years were not all that she would achieve. But she felt she was wrong. In her journey of truth she had found it was inside her all along.

This was it. The highest point of her life being spent on the highest point on the planet. What did she expect? A flood of faith? Or the voice of God? Nothing, she had expected meaning, purpose. She could not see what more she could achieve she could not go back, her overwhelming urge was that if she did, it would be downhill, she could never get higher. She pitched herself forward and launched herself into oblivion. With the rush of wind she closed her eyes and prepared for the eternal adventure, the only place left for her to go, either higher than high, or way down below. Which way she did not care.

10 DEAD

My skin undulates with the infestation living beneath it. It creeps, it crawls, and it breaths and grows. The fear is not there, I should be terrified that something is taking over the very marrow of my bones. I feel nothing. It is confusing, surely these abominations inside me should make me feel something? The movement is not my muscles tensing and contracting, it is purely those parasites that feed off me.
Why should I care? After all, I have been dead for weeks. I just don't feel the urge to move, not with my body still lying here, putrefying.

11 NIGHT TERROR

Under normal circumstances the sheet from his bed wrapped around Edwin's legs would have been enough to wake him. He was a constant nocturnal mover. Even the sweat burn caused by the sheets extra insulation was the cause for his awakening tonight.

There was a noise out in the night, unless of course he dreamt it, that maybe/maybe not feeling of being woken in the middle of the night. He lay still, wide awake now. Ed was almost holding his breath waiting for confirmation with a reoccurrence of the sound through the night air.

Ed didn't have to wait long as a long, drawn out cry disturbed the peace. Lying in bed, inside his house, he could not place where in suburbia the sound was emanating. It could have been half a mile away in the silence of the early hour. Equally it could have been from his neighbouring property.

He untangled himself from the bedding, got up, and peered past the curtain of the partially open window. Again, the sound was heard off to his right. He at least now knew the direction, but still he was unable to pinpoint how near or far away it was.

He tried to peer sideways through the glass, only seeing as far as the halcyon glow of the streetlight would allow. Another howl, this time ending with an anguished crying broke the silence again. Ed glanced back at the clock, the luminous figures displaying that it was just past three am. He was torn between having a look, going back to bed or calling someone. He knew if he ignored it he would regret it if there really was something bad happening, the last thing he wanted was a copper knocking on the door in the morning asking if he had seen or heard something suspicious in the night.

Another scream finally decided his action. He rescued his top and denims from the floor where he had dumped them the night before. After pulling them on he jogged down the stairs and pulled on a pair of trainers from under the coat stand in the hall.

He headed towards the kitchen. Ed stopped at the utility room on his way past. On the floor, just inside the doorway, sat his battered metal flake blue toolbox. He flipped the lid, he raised his eyebrows and smiled as he picked up a ball peen hammer, holding it firmly and gave it a quick shake. It would not hurt to have some protection, after all he didn't really know what he was getting himself into. With his free hand, he took a penlight from the toolbox.

He flicked the penlight on and off to check the batteries then slipped it into his pocket. He made for the back door. The cool night air took his breath away for a moment and sent a chill through him. He briefly glanced at his steel barred dog pen and noticed the door was ajar as he left by the rear gate.

He walked with purpose along the side of his house and out into the deserted street. The silence was eerie. Ed stood, the hammer hanging to his side. He immediately shot his head to the right as another cry broke the air with an echo.

Ed now had an idea where the sound was emanating from. As he walked along the road towards the small patch of wasteland he noted that not a single light emanated from any of his adjacent properties. He felt a little alone, not an unknown concept to him, but out here tonight it was a little intimidating.

He approached the drop kerb that heralded the rough entrance to the churned up piece of land. It was a small area, but before long it would be built on with half a dozen small properties, he had seen the planning request.

Ed stood staring through the dusky darkness. The cry, although lower in volume, was just ahead of him. He pulled the penlight from his pocket and moved cautiously scanning just ahead of him to ensure of a good footing through the rough landscape.

He stopped just mere inches from the crawling figure of what looked like a young woman. Her scant clothing was moist and heavily stained, she sobbed as she pulled herself along. Her useless ragged feet dragged along behind her mingling dirt and blood.

With the torchlight shining on her face she turned to look at him. Her face was slick with tears and spittle as she sobbed, lank matted mousey hair stuck to her cheek.

"Help me." She squeaked.

Ed looked down at her, all fear now gone.

"You got some heart young lady, without your toes I never though you would ever try to run away."

Her eyes widened as she recognised the voice of her captor. The man she had fancied, the man who turned out to be a predator, a dangerous animal. She opened her mouth, but the hammer silenced her before the scream escaped.

Ed dropped the blood-soaked hammer into the kitchen sink with a clatter and turned on the faucet. He ran his hands under the tap and wrung them together to remove the worst of the gore. Using a tea towel he dried his hands as he crossed the kitchen and jostled the mouse next to the laptop that was situated there.

"Next!" He scowled as he began to create another dating profile online.

12 ABANDONED LUGGAGE

If it could, the lonely battered suitcase would weep. The lost luggage warehouse was not a nice place for a small one like him. It was cold, sitting on the shelf waiting for his owner. She was a nice little girl and her toys were locked within.

People passed by, but they barely batted an eyelid in his direction. Just as he was about to give up hope and throw himself from the shelf, some wanderers appeared. They looked familiar. A small child looked in his direction. Her face broke into a wide smile as her eyes met with him.

13 DIVIDED BUT UNITED

Two elderly gentlemen sat in the glazed conservatory of the nursing home. This was their place. They had never met prior to the last two years that they had been there, but they had struck up a firm friendship the first day they chose their positions in the conservatory attached to the day room, the very same place where they were sitting now.

Both were of similar age and they often chatted about the old days. A time when they had been fit, able and still learning about the ways of the world.

The time had come where they had learnt as much as they were going to, reminiscence was the order of the day and their memories were all that they had left.

Arthur jostled his wheelchair around slightly so as to get a better view of the countryside outside the window. Having been a farmhand for the majority of his life he so missed actually being out in it. He settled back with his thoughts.

Harry was sitting back in his chair fingers latticed in his lap twirling his thumbs around each other.

"Tea up." Came the hearty call from the day room.

Harry leaned forward, "Usual Arthur?" He enquired.

As if dragged suddenly from his thoughts Arthur turned and faced his friend.

"Oh yes please. I think I'll have a biscuit or two as well today."

Harry smiled and pushed himself up from his chair with a groan. He limped from the room into the adjoining spacious day room. Josie, the ample bosomed helper, was standing at the urn on its trolley.

The room was sparse but comfortable. This particular day there were just a handful of residents dotted around in high backed chairs. Josie smiled as Harry approached her.

"Two cups of tea, one with sweetener?" She enquired with a smile.

"Yes please, I am so predictable." He shook his head.

She giggled and prepared the beverages.

"Oh and a couple of malted milks for Arthur please." He added

Her smile was a little more strained at the mention of his friend. She placed two biscuits in the saucer of the cup with sweetener then placed both on a small tray.

"Are you okay with that Harold?" Josie had a habit of calling people by their full moniker, respect that Harry and the other residents appreciated in this day and age, it gave an air of respect for ones elders.

He gratefully thanked her and took the tray. The journey back was with less of a limp, he felt it eased when he exercised it a little. Unfortunately his angina restricted exercise to no more than the trip from his room to the conservatory. Stuck in a chair all day stiffened his joints.

He placed the cup and biscuits on the window sill next to his friend. Arthur looked up startled from a little world of his own.

"Oh, thank you my friend," Arthur said flustered.

Harry re-took his seat opposite and groaned as he sat down.

"You were miles away then mate." Harry said.

Arthur rubbed his forehead, a pained expression on his face.

"Just reminiscing to myself, if you can call it that." He shrugged.

"What's up Arthur?" Harry asked with genuine concern.

"Can I ask you something?" Arthur leaned forward.

"Of course Art, we've known each other long enough." Harry smiled.

"Have you ever killed anyone?" Arthur asked in a normal tone of voice..

Harry paused a little stunned and somewhat taken aback.

They had talked about everything over the years, even his military service. Arthur knew he had served a tour in Northern Ireland, but had never pushed him on the subject. Harry looked down at his lap.

"I'm not proud of the things that happened in NI. It was a turbulent time and I was young and impudent." He said quietly, he then looked up into Arthurs' face. His friend was looking back at him with an air of forgiving.

"It certainly was. You know I grew up in the Republic, it was all over." He nodded.

"I didn't think they were affected so much down South." Harry said surprised knowing his friend originally hailed from Southern Ireland.

"Well, I have to admit I lied to you a little, and for that I must apologise."

Harry looked at Arthur a little perplexed and suspicious.

"I was born in the Republic, most of us were, but I spent most of my formative years in Belfast." He smiled.

"You never said?" Replied Harry surprised.

Arthur moved forward as far as his chair would allow and he patted Harry's knee.

"I never needed to tell you this tale before until now, the time is drawing near." His eyes sparkled as if he were an excited child desperate to tell a secret. Harry leaned forward interested, but a little dubious. His time stationed close to Belfast still gave him occasional sleepless nights.

"When you're young," Arthur began "You're an empty vessel and you do things, eager to fill that vessel, things that aren't necessarily what you would chose. It's not by choice, it's purely circumstance, peer pressure even."

Harry unconsciously nodded his agreement.

"I was mixing with people who had radical ideas, and good or bad, I joined in." The realization dawned on Harry. They had fought on opposite sides, he was starting to feel worried, concerned that their differences could ruin the friendship that they had built up.

"No need to worry about our friendship, its solid." Said Arthur as if reading his mind.

"I did some bad things back then." Harry rubbed

his forehead with a shaky hand.

"There was one in particular that I do regret."

"I know" said Arthur soothingly "You can talk to me, I want to hear your story."

For a long time Harry had wanted to tell someone, anyone. He had no family, no friends, plenty of acquaintances but nobody close enough to confide in. Arthur was his closest friend despite having known him only a couple of years. Now knowing that this friend had served in the same conflict meant that Arthur was likely to understand better than most.

"I'll ask my original question again," said Arthur, slowing his speech as if talking to a petulant child "Have you ever killed anyone?"

The straightforward way in which he asked the question, he could have made a good psychiatrist Harry thought. He rubbed his face and sighed, then placed his hands in his lap to compose himself.

"Yes." He said clearly with conviction.

"You've never told anyone, have you" Arthur stated this as if he already knew the answer.

"I've carried the guilt with me for a long time." Harry said quietly. "Never a day goes by that I don't think about the lives I took."

"What happened in your eyes?" Asked Arthur.

Harry looked up into the space above Arthurs head. He had thought about what happened countless times over the years, but never had to recount the story since the original enquiry.

"I was a private in Her Majesty's Army, I spent most of my tour at the border checkpoints." He began. "It was a misty night, we were on alert because we had just been told the latest round of peace talks had just fallen through. It generally meant trouble when that happened. There were only two of us on the border, it wasn't a busy one. That night I was with my corporal, Jason Knights. He was okay, we'd been drunk together on more than one occasion." He managed a choked laugh when he recalled.

"At around 0200 hours, a car approached." Harry Swallowed "We were on edge of course, there had been reports of sporadic violence all over Belfast. The car seemed to just keep coming, appearing not to slow up for the checkpoint. Jason turned on the spotlights and joined me up at the barrier. We had those damned heavy self-loading rifles at the time, weighed a ton, but really powerful." He paused to swallow. "The car still didn't slow up." He shook his head, the tenseness of the situation coming back to him. "We had no choice, we had to open fire. He held his face in his hands again.

"What happened then?" Arthur queried respectfully.

"The 7.62 mil rounds ripped the car apart, it slid and swerved, a round must have rupture the fuel tank, the car was obliterated, both Jason and myself ended up in hospital from the blast." Harry had tears in his eyes.

"Two of the three occupants died by our bullets, the third died in the explosion. If it hadn't come out that they were all innocents, it might have been easier to bear." He sobbed.

"What do you mean, innocents?" Asked Arthur with a slightly perplexed expression.

"They were just friends coming back from a trip to see relatives down South." Harry replied.

Arthur burst into hysterical laughter. Harry pulled back into his chair shocked at his friends' jovial outburst. Arthur pointed at Harry,

"You thought they were innocent." He stammered as he bawled.

"What? ... but, but they were." Harry said.

Arthur stopped in mid laugh becoming instantly straight faced.

"We were not innocent." Arthur said slowly and sternly. "You thought for all those years that you had murdered innocent people, but you are wrong."

Harry sat stunned mouth agape.

"The plan was that we drive up to the checkpoint then torch the car with road flares, us and the car were soaked in petrol, you hit us too soon, you were doing your job. And that night you did a good job."

"But nobody survived, how could you have been there?" Said Harry exasperated.

"I was in the thick of it my friend, I was driving, and I took two of your bullets, and one of your Corporals." Arthur smiled.

"What are you then, some sort of ghost?" Questioned Harry.

"Of sorts." He breathed heavily before he continued. "Heaven and Hell aren't for the likes of us my friend. When the likes of us die we expect to go to hell, but it's not that cut and dried."

Harry felt overly tired, but was transfixed by what his pal had to say.

"The Vikings probably had it closest with their Valhalla. We are misplaced, we are segregated from good and evil, we are somewhere in the middle." Arthur pronounced.

"So why are you here? Why now?" Harry asked.

"When your times up, your times up, your time is up my friend. I'm here as your ticket to Valhalla."

Arthur chortled.

"But I killed you, why should you care?" Said Harry his face lolling slightly to the side.

"I have been your guardian angel ever since I left this world. When you reach Valhalla, hate, fear, ideals, class, race, creed, colour all disappear when you go. Pity and compassion still remain. I pitied you, I watched you weep for hours over me and my compatriots, and I felt responsible."

"I never forgave myself." Harry slurred finding it difficult to find his words.

"Well now you can end all the pain, time to drop this shit life." Arthur stood and stretched out his hands. "Time to go soldier, got some people you should meet and some sights to show you."

Harry closed his eyes.

***

As night fell over the nursing home only one of the old pals remained seated gazing out of the conservatory into the night. The entire day room was empty.

Josie passed through the dull room, pulling on her coat as she bustled on through. She stopped as she noticed the figure still seated now the other residents had retired. Her care for the residents overshadowed any plans she may have had at the end of her shift.

"Harold?" She called "What are you doing? It's late."

He did not reply or move. Josie went over, the concern etched across her face was genuine, and she truly liked this old man. Arthur sat staring with unseeing eyes at his own reflection in the darkened glazing. Josie dropped her handbag and discarded her coat by the chair and immediately started hunting for a pulse on the cool flesh of Harry's neck.

From outside, in the darkness at the edge of the grounds, two figures watched as Josie rushed around using all her medical knowledge to try and revive the old man. More carers appeared to aid her.

The two shadows turned and walked together away from the home.

"See Harry, I told you it would be far less painful than living."

Harry nodded, "I'll miss Josie's tea." he smiled.

As they walked their agedness dissipated, they walked tall and solid. They faded as their appearance became younger, within seconds they finally disappeared into the ether.

14 NO JOB SATISFACTION

Tommy hated his job, the hours were crap, the tools of the trade were archaic to say the least. Job satisfaction was nil, not like he got paid for it.

An eternity of community service was the way he saw it. Even the customers were never happy.

He would hand in his notice but his employer wasn't the most forgiving, his son was, but sadly he wasn't in charge.

It always seems so easy looking from the outside in, but in reality, his job was menial, repetitive and boring. Being the Grim Reaper was the most depressing job in existence.

15 DAWN OF THE TRIFFIDS

David fervently tore open the envelope that the postman had just delivered. Inside he unfolded the letter and read quickly. He collapsed to his knees, leant back with his fists punching air like he'd just scored the winning try for the England Rugby team. "Yeessss" he shouted "I got the job"

David had been working for his current Bank for many years and was desperate to get a foot in the private sector. Triffoil was fast becoming a major player in the fuel oil industry, despite the secrecy surrounding its production. The wage in his current position was miniscule compared to the pay and benefits offered by this up and coming new company.

The next few weeks dragged laboriously, the same old faces at the teller's desk and the same clock hands moving slower and slower to that five o'clock deadline.

The day finally arrived. David dressed smartly and

after a light breakfast waited to be collected as the company had arranged. Right on time a Range Rover pulled up to the kerb outside his house. One quick adjustment of his tie in the hallway mirror and he left the house, as he approached the car a smartly dressed man walked around from the driver's side and approached him hand outstretched. "Good morning Mr Moody, my name is Mac Kinnon and I'll be taking you to the farm this morning." David shook his hand "David, please call me David," he replied.

The farm was only twenty minutes' drive from David's home, Mac was congenial he was a general goffer for the local Triffoil farm, David warmed to him. They turned off the main road and continued on a single lane track sided with woodland, after a few hundred yards they approached what resembled a military checkpoint. Mac slowed the car as a security guard approached them from the small hut. Mac lowered the window; the guard on duty recognised Mac and waved them through. After a short run they pulled up into a small car park opposite an office building. Beyond that the acres of secure compound stuffed with green and yellow plants, Triffids.

They left the car and Mac led David towards the innocuous entrance. As they approached a young woman in a lab coat was shouldering the door open with arms piled high with folders. He could see straight away that her angle of exit was off balance and was going to end in tears. Quickening his pace he reached for the door hoping to overt disaster, but alas by pulling the door open for her actually made her lose balance and as predicted the files flew from her arms with a splat on the concrete step.

"I am so sorry," he proffered whilst kneeling to

retrieve the folders.

"Hi Rebecca, this is David Moody the new accounts guy," Mac said.

"Should be David Clumsy," she retorted sarcastically. "He doesn't look moody, are you sure you got the right person this time"

"How was I to know they were wrong? They were waiting in the right place."

"For one thing how many Japanese men are called Rachel?"

David smirked like a schoolboy scoffing at another's prank on the teacher. For the briefest second Rebecca flashed a quick smile and whisked away continuing her journey to her car. "Aw man," Mac whined "she's always ragging on me"

"In that case it might be true love."

"Do you really think so?" Mac said with a hopeful lilt in his voice. David laughed.

David settled in his new position quickly. He found the work itself well within his abilities and the rest of the small team incredibly friendly. Even Rebecca's frosty exterior had thawed somewhat. He was also fascinated by the nature of the plant they were harvesting.

The triffids themselves were relatively safe. The poison glands had to remain as removal affected the quality of the oil product tapped from their root bolls. Every aspect of safety was adhered to, despite that accidents did happen. A little earlier Bill one of the leading technicians was caught out by a juvenile plant. The force of the sting was enough to dislodge his mask allowing a small amount of venom into his eyes, blinding him. Reports from the hospital were good and due to the young age of the plant thankfully the poison was not to full potency, as such the blindness would be temporary. That was good news as Bill was a good bloke and had a real passion for his job.

Most lunch breaks David took a wander around the compound. Despite their danger he was totally safe behind the electrified fence. He had a great deal of respect for the plants they earned a substantial amount of money for the minimal overheads involved.

As David walked he realised there was a triffid seedling outside the fencing. It was unusual to find a juvenile outside as the paths were scrubbed on a daily basis to prevent such an occurrence. He leant down and inspected the small seedling; it just looked like a miniature version of the adult. Then David had a flash of impetuousness, he glanced around then took his empty lunch box from his bag. He plucked the plant from the path and gently placed it in the box. After replacing his lunchbox back in his bag he quickly scanned around and continued his walk.

When he arrived home he tentatively opened the lunchbox. The young triffid looked a little limp. He took an old plant off the kitchen window sill after discarding the current occupant he replanted the seedling in the pot. He watered it and placed it on the sill admiringly.

David tended the plant daily, after re-potting several times the conservatory became the triffids new home. At five feet tall normal plant feed just wasn't enough, but thankfully there was an abundance of small mammals scurrying around the unkempt back garden, nearly as many as the numerous traps around the garden to ensnare them.

As the days became weeks so to the triffid grew to maturity. David found a name for his plant, Triffy. Despite not being able to fetch sticks and play ball she was treated as a pet and companion. David spent many evenings in the conservatory relaxing and reading out loud to Triffy. She never ever tried to attack David, a mutual friendship and respect had grown between them.

David never had very many visitors and so when the doorbell rang he jumped. He went to the front door and opened it. "Dave, sorry to bother you, I've broken down around the corner can I borrow your phone?" Said Mac. "Yes of course" he opened the door wider and turned pulling the kitchen door to, hoping Mac couldn't see through to the conservatory. He gestured towards the phone on the small hallway table. "Cheers mate, you're a godsend," Mac said as he picked up the receiver. Unnoticed by David as he went back to close the front door the kitchen door blew open slightly. As he turned back to Mac he saw Triffy's stinger flash through the open door way hitting Mac full in the face. He collapsed onto the table and rolled onto the floor at David's feet. Mac was dead; having never been de-sacked Triffy's poison was excessively potent.

David rushed through to the conservatory where he found Triffy had uprooted herself and was facing through the doorway. "You bad, bad girl," he said angrily, then realised he was telling off a rather deadly plant, he backed up a little. Then it dawned that Triffy wasn't going to hit out at him, he had actually tamed a triffid. As he gently stroked her stalk she edged back to her position in the conservatory. "Oh well, waste not want not"

That evening David stripped off Macs corpse and dissected his body into smaller portions laying some in front of Triffy. He knew that sort of feed would last quite some time.

Work was still ticking along; he was briefly interviewed by the police. Apparently Mac had gone missing and they spoke to everyone who knew him.

Later that week David was as usual enjoying his free time reading to Triffy, he'd noticed a few flashes in the night sky, He thought maybe there was a thunderstorm going on somewhere near. Then the doorbell rang. He turned off the light in the conservatory and pulled to the door behind him.

This time he made sure the kitchen door was shut as he headed for the front door and opened it. "Rebecca. What are you doing here?" He said genuinely surprised.

"Sorry to bother you David, I just wanted to see if you were okay"

Perplexed he said, "of course I am, what are you on about?"

"Can I come in?" She asked

"Of course where are my manners, please," David closed the door behind her and led her through to the kitchen, as he went in he pulled the conservatory door closed. Rebecca sat at the table while David busied himself with the kettle. "So what's up?"

Rebecca continued "Didn't the police tell you they suspect Mac's disappearance is possibly the act of environmentalists."

"Not at all," he replied

"It just got me scared; I didn't want to be on my own."

"That surprises me I thought you were tough as

nails," he said as he prepared two mugs of coffee.

"It's a bit of a defence mechanism, it's not easy working in a predominantly male organisation when it comes down to it I'm still only a woman."

As I took the mugs over to the table there was a bumping sound coming from the door to the conservatory. "Have you got a dog David? You never said." Rebecca caught him off guard and quickly stood up heading for the door, "Don't…"

But it was too late. As quickly as she opened the door Triffy hit her point blank in the face throwing her backwards across the kitchen and into the hallway. David's head dropped into his hands. He dragged Rebecca's lifeless body into the conservatory and dropped into his chair.

"Triffy, what are you turning me into?"

The flashes in the sky were becoming more prevalent as the large meteor shower burned up as it entered our atmosphere causing an incredibly beautiful air display. David standing next to Triffy gazed out at the spectacle and only barely acknowledged as the spade swung through the air beheading Triffy and knocking him to the floor, he turned over and looked into Rebecca's heavy mutilated face

"I knew it was you," she shouted" I saw you pick up that rogue plant."

The right side of her face was a mass of raw meat, her eye missing she must have turned her face as Triffy hit her as the left eye looked fine "You've killed me, I know how this stuff works remember. Within hours I'll be dead, and if you'd had your way I'd be triffid food but it isn't going to happen."

She raised the spade, but David was faster he

jumped up and pushed Rebecca to the other side of the conservatory pushing her head hard into the reinforced glass. He continued until her body dropped to the floor. This time he checked her pulse before turning his back on her. "Oh Triffy!" The decapitated plant was dead. David was disappointed but not as cut up as he'd thought he'd be. He grabbed Rebecca's corpse under the arms and dragged her through to the living room. Leaving her in the middle of the floor he turned back and turned on the light.

"Dinner up boys and girls," he said to the half a dozen triffids in the room, he really was becoming the cat lady of triffids he thought to himself. On his way up to bed he had the most wretched of headaches. Oh well, tomorrow's another day.

ABOUT THE AUTHOR

Paul S. Huggins hails from the United Kingdom on the history and witchcraft rich Essex coast. There he resides with his muse and partner in crime, Sally. His introduction to the horror genre was being scared to death at an early age by a movie called 'Dawn of the Dead'. It changed his whole aspect on the apocalypse, and now thinks when not if! Nowadays his jottings have moved from the undead to some things for more ethereal and sometimes virus ridden. With thirteen short stories published in various anthologies and five self-published books, Paul would say horror is in his blood, but thankfully, he is still living.

Printed in Poland
by Amazon Fulfillment
Poland Sp. z o.o., Wrocław